To my lola Soling,
who let me eat all the candy

First edition 2023

Library of Congress Catalog Card Number 2022907293
ISBN 978-1-5362-2614-0

23 24 25 26 27 28 CCP 10 9 8 7 6 5 4 3 2 1

Printed in Shenzhen, Guangdong, China

This book was typeset in Sweater School and Neucha.
The illustrations were created digitally.

Candlewick Press
99 Dover Street
Somerville, Massachusetts 02144

www.candlewick.com

SARI-SARI SUMMERS

LYNNOR BONTIGAO

CANDLEWICK PRESS

Nora loves spending summers with her lola.

"You've gotten so big, my apo!" says Lola.

The mango tree they planted outside the sari-sari store has gotten bigger, too, with green fruit hanging from the branches.

The streets around Lola's sari-sari store are loud and colorful. The motorcycles zig and zag their way into traffic while the sweet smell of warm soft tofu, caramel syrup, and tapioca pearls fills the air.

This year, Nora is big enough to help
at the sari-sari store.

You can buy ANYTHING there! Hair clips, salty kropek, condiments, toys, detergents in small

packets, creamy yema, sour tamarind candy,
mung beans, komiks, and all kinds of treats!

Nora is a big help to her lola.

She cleans . . .

refills . . .

and sorts.

But her favorite job is measuring.

"One small scoop of rice for Mrs. Cruz, two BIG scoops of beans for Mr. Tan."

Lola says, "Give them extra. They're my best customers, my suki." Nora is careful not to spill.

But one day, no one comes to the store.

"Don't worry, Nora. I think it's just too hot today.
They'll come tomorrow," says Lola.

But the next day is another hot day.

So is the day after that and the day after that.

If no one comes, Nora won't be refilling, sorting, or measuring.

What if Lola doesn't need my help at the store anymore?

What if Lola sends me back home?

What if we don't spend the rest of the summer together?

HEAT WAVE

"Let's get some fresh air, my apo," Lola says.

Resting under the mango tree, Nora
sees something that cheers her up.

"Lola, the mangoes are ripe!

Maybe we can make
ICE CANDY!"

Lola smiles.

"That sounds like
a great idea, hija."

That afternoon, Lola and Nora
make ice candy in their kitchen.

Lola cuts the mango
and scoops out the
golden fruit.

Nora pours the condensed milk and cream.

Mix! Mix! MIX!

"Needs more milk." Nora tastes again.

"Too sweet!" Nora adds more cream.

"How does it taste?" Lola asks.

Both Nora and her lola want to drink it like juice, but Lola says they have to freeze it first.

The next morning, it is still hot and the sari-sari store is still empty, but Nora isn't worried anymore. Nora and Lola have a plan.

ICE CANDY

MANGO
COCONUT
MELON
AVOCADO

It's a hit!

The next day, Nora and her lola go
to the market to buy more fruit—
coconut, melon, avocado.

People come back every day for the
ice candy and more.

Mrs. Cruz asks for avocado ice
candy and two big scoops of rice.

Mr. Tan buys the coconut flavor
and an extra scoop of beans.

Nora gets to measure again!

Before Nora leaves to go home, Nora and Lola share the last of the ice candies.

"Ah, this really cools me down," Lola says. "Thank you for your help, my apo. Because of you, the sari-sari store did really well this summer. Salamat."

Nora puts her arms around her, smells
her cheeks between kisses, and
asks, "Do you know one thing I can't
measure, Lola? How much I love you!"

Soling's Ice Candy Recipe

3-4 ripe mangoes*
1 can condensed milk
1 can evaporated milk
1 can table cream
  ice candy bags

Tools: Blender and funnel

* You can use other fruit: avocado, coconut, ube, melon, etc.

Scoop out mangoes into blender.
Add the rest of the ingredients.
Blend until smooth.
Pour into ice candy bags using funnel.
Tie ends tightly.
Freeze and enjoy!